THE STORY OF
A CHINA CAT

LAURA LEE HOPE

THE STORY OF A CHINA CAT

CHAPTER I

TOY-SHOP FUN

Toot! Toot! Tootity-toot-toot!

"Goodness me! who is blowing the horn?" asked the Talking Doll, as she sat up on the shelf in the toy shop. "This isn't Friday; and we don't want any fish!"

"Speak for yourself, if you please," said a large, white China Cat, who had just finished washing a few specks of dirt off her shiny coat with her red tongue. "I could enjoy a bit of fish right now."

"I should rather have pie," said the Talking Doll. "But who blew the horn? That is what I'd like to know. No one has a horn in this toy shop that I know anything about."

"It wasn't a horn—that was a trumpet," said another voice. "I'll blow it again!"

Then there sounded a jolly noise through the quiet toy shop, which was in darkness except for one electric light in the middle of the store.

Toot! Toot! Tootity-toot-toot! echoed the merry notes.

"What a pretty sound," said the Jumping Jack, as he jerked his arms and legs up and down, for he had just awakened from his long day of sleep.

"Isn't it nice," agreed Tumbling Tom, a queer toy who never could stand up, because he was made in such a funny way that he always fell down. "I wonder if there is going to be a parade?"

"Who is blowing that horn, anyway?" asked the Talking Doll.

"I tell you it isn't a horn—it's a trumpet, and I am blowing it," said a voice in the front part of the toy store. "I came in only to-day, but I thought perhaps you other toys would like a little music, so I tuned up my trumpet. But please don't call it a horn. I am not a fish man!"

With that there came walking along the shelf, from the front part of the store, a little man wearing a blue coat, dark red trousers, and a hat with a long, sweeping plume. I say he was a little man, but I mean he was a toy, dressed up like a man such as you see in fairy stories. In his hand he carried a little golden trumpet.

As he walked along the shelf, where the other toys stood, the Trumpeter, for such he was, blew another blast on his golden instrument.

And the blast was such a jolly one that every toy in the store felt like dancing or singing. The Jumping Jack worked his arms and legs faster than they had ever jerked about before. The Talking Doll swayed on her feet as though waltzing, and even the China Cat beat time with her tail.

"That certainly was very nice," said the Talking Doll, when the Trumpeter had finished the tune. "Did you say you just came here to be one of us?"

"Just to-day," was the answer. "I came in a large box, straight from the workshop of Santa Claus, at the North Pole, and I—"

"Oh! The North Pole!" suddenly mewed the China Cat.

"What's the matter? Does it make you chilly to hear about the North Pole, where I came from?" asked the Trumpeter.

"No," answered the Cat. "I was just thinking of a friend of mine who once lived there. You remember him," she added, turning to the Jumping Jack. "I mean the Nodding Donkey."

"Of course I remember him!" said the Jumping Jack. "I should say I did! A most jolly chap, always bowing to you in the most friendly way. He isn't here any more."

"No, he was bought for a little lame boy who had to go on crutches," said the Talking Doll. "I remember the Nodding Donkey very well. I say he was bought for a little lame boy. But the truth of the matter is that the lame boy got well, and now is just like other boys. Once the Nodding Donkey's leg was broken and he was brought back here for Mr. Mugg to fix."

"Who is Mr. Mugg?" asked the Trumpeter, as he rubbed his horn to make it more shiny. "Excuse me for asking, but I have not been here very long, you know," he added.

"Mr. Horatio Mugg is the man who keeps this toy store," explained the China Cat. "He and his daughters, Angelina and Geraldine, keep us toys in order, dust us off and sell us whenever any one comes in to buy playthings."

"Then it seems I am not to stay here always," went on the Trumpeter. "Well, I like a jolly life, going about from place to place. I had fun at the North Pole, and now I hope I shall have some fun here. That's why I blew my trumpet— to start you toys into life."

"We always come to life after dark, and make believe we are alive when no one sees us," explained the China Cat. "That is one of the things we are allowed to do. But as soon as daylight shines, or when any one comes into the store to look at us, we must turn back into toys that can move only when we are wound up. That is, all except me. I have no springs inside me—

I move of myself whenever make-believe time comes," she added, and she switched her tail from side to side.

"Well, I have springs inside me," said the Talking Doll, "and also a little phonograph. When it is wound up I can say 'papa' and 'mama' and 'I am hungry.' But when we are by ourselves, as we are now, I can say what I please."

"I, too, have springs inside me," said the Trumpeter. "That is how I blow my trumpet. But now, as we are by ourselves and it is night, why not have some fun? Let's do something. Perhaps, as a newcomer, I should let some one else start it. But I could not bear to lie on the shelf, doing nothing, especially when it is so near the jolly Christmas season. So I just blew my trumpet to awaken you all."

"And I'm glad you did," said the Jumping Jack. "I say let's have some fun! Shall I show you how well I can jump?" he asked. "If this is your first night here," he said to the Trumpeter, "you do not know all the tricks I can do."

"I should be most happy to see you do some," replied the Trumpeter.

"Oh, that Jumping Jack. He thinks he is the only one who can jump!" whispered a Jack in the Box to Tumbling Tom. "If I could get out of this box I'd show him some jumps that would make him open his eyes!"

"And as for tumbles!" said Tom. "Why, I can beat him all to pieces! But we must be polite, you know, especially before strangers—I mean the Trumpeter. Don't let's have a quarrel."

"All right," agreed the Jack in the Box, or Jack Box, as he was called for short.

"Now watch me jump!" cried Jumping Jack. "Clear the shelf, if you please. The Trumpeter has never seen any of my circus tricks!"

So the toys in the shop of Mr. Horatio Mugg got ready to have a jolly night. Just as the China Cat had said, the toys had the power of making believe. They could pretend to come to life, and talk among themselves, and do things they never would think of doing in the daytime. This was when no human eyes saw them.

"Attention now, everybody!" called the Jumping Jack, just like the ringmaster in a circus. "First I will climb to the top of the highest shelf, and then I will jump down."

"Won't you hurt yourself?" asked the Trumpeter.

"Oh, no, I'll land on a big rubber ball and bounce," the Jumping Jack answered. "If you want to, Trumpeter," he added, "you can blow a blast on your horn to start me off. It will be more exciting if you do that."

"All right," agreed the new toy.

Up climbed the Jumping Jack until he stood on the very highest shelf of the store—the shelf where all the extra drums were kept out of the way.

"It makes me dizzy to look at him," said the Talking Doll, and she covered her eyes with her hand.

"Yes, suppose he should fall," said the China Cat. "But he must show off, I suppose. I'd rather have less exciting fun—such as a game of tag."

"Hush!" begged the Trumpeter. "He is ready to jump, I think. Hello there, Jack!" he called to the toy on the top shelf. "Are you ready?"

"All ready!" was the answer. "Blow your trumpet, and I'll jump!"

The Trumpeter raised his golden horn to his lips.

Toot! Toot! Tootity-toot-toot! came the blast.

"Here I come!" shouted the Jumping Jack.

"Oh, dear! Tell me when it is all over!" begged the Talking Doll, putting both her hands over her eyes.

Down, down, down, came the Jumping Jack, past shelf after shelf of toys, until he landed with a bounce on a rubber ball on the very lowest shelf, where the Cat and the Doll stood.

Up in the air bounced the Jack again, for the ball was like the springs of a bed. Then he came down upon the ball a second time and bounced up once more, and this time he came down on the shelf.

"Ouch! Mew! Mew!" cried the China Cat.

"What's the matter? Did the Jumping Jack fall and break his leg like the Nodding Donkey?" asked the Talking Doll. "Oh, I dare not look! Tell me about it!"

"Of course he didn't break his leg!" said the Cat. "But he stepped on my tail; that's what he did! Right on my tail! I hope it isn't broken," she went on, as she looked carefully at the tip.

"Oh, I beg your pardon! I am so sorry!" exclaimed the Jumping Jack. "I didn't mean to do that. The ball rolled, and I slipped."

"Well, there is no great harm done, I am glad to say," said the China Cat, again carefully looking at the tip of her tail. "But if you had landed a little harder you would have broken it, and then I should be a damaged toy, and Mr. Mugg would have had to sell me for half price."

"But didn't I do a good jump?" asked the Jack of the Trumpeter.

"One of the finest I ever saw," was the answer. "But suppose we play something more quiet."

"Let's have a dance!" proposed the Talking Doll. "The Trumpeter can play for us. I love to dance!"

"So do I," said a Soldier Captain, who was one of a number of wooden soldiers in a box. "May I have a waltz with you, Miss Doll?"

"Yes," she answered. "Thank you, Captain."

And while the Trumpeter played, the toys danced. The Jumping Jack danced with the China Cat, but she said his style was jerky. Then Tumbling Tom danced with the white cat, but Tom kept falling down all the while so that dance was, really, not a success.

"Let's play tag," said the Talking Doll after a while. "I am sure the Trumpeter is tired of playing so many tunes for us."

"All right! Tag will be fun!" agreed the China Cat. "I'll be it. Scatter now, so I shall have to run to tag you."

The toys spread themselves about the shelves of Mr. Mugg's shop, and the China Cat, whose shiny coat was as white as snow, was just getting ready to run after the Trumpeter when suddenly the toy pussy gave a loud mew.

"Take her away! Take her away! Don't let her come near me!" cried the China Cat. "Oh, Captain!" she exclaimed to the wooden soldier, "don't let her get near me! Take her away!" and the China Cat acted so strangely that the other toys did not know what to think.

CHAPTER II

A NICE LITTLE GIRL

Everybody had been so happy and jolly in the toy shop, and there was so much fun going on, that when the China Cat acted so oddly and mewed so loudly, there was great excitement for a time.

"Don't tell me there is a fire!" cried a little Ballet Dancer, whose skirts of tissue paper and tulle would be sure to flare up the first thing in case of a blaze.

"No, there isn't a fire," said a toy Policeman. "If there was I should turn in an alarm."

"But what is the matter?" asked the Talking Doll. "Did that crazy Jumping Jack again step on the China Cat's tail?"

"Indeed I did not," answered the Jumping Jack.

And all this while the China Cat kept mewing.

"Take her away! Don't let her come near me! The black will rub off, I'm sure, and I shall be ruined and damaged. Oh, take her away, Soldier Captain!" and the China Cat, in her white coat, snuggled as close as she could to the brave officer with his shiny sword.

"What is the matter? Who is black? Please tell me what to do so I can help you," begged the Captain.

"Why, don't you see!" exclaimed the China Cat. "That black doll is coming to play tag with us! She belongs on the other side of the store, among the Hallowe'en novelties! If she rubs up against me she'll get me all black, and I can't stand it to be dirty!"

All the other toys glanced toward the toy at which the China Cat pointed with one paw. Walking along the edge of the shelf was a fuzzy-haired black Doll, her face as shiny as the stove pipe. She was called a Topsy Doll.

"Whut's de mattah heah?" asked Topsy, talking just as a colored doll should talk. "Don't yo' all want fo' me to come an' play tag wif yo'?"

"We'd love to have you," said the Jumping Jack, who, being all sorts of colors, did not mind one more. "But our China Cat is afraid some of your black might rub off on her."

"Ha! Ha! Ha!" laughed Topsy. "Dat suah am funny! Why, my black doesn't come off! I spects maybe I's white inside, but de black on de outside don't come off! Ha! Ha! Ha!"

8

"Really, doesn't it? Won't you smut me all up?" asked the China Cat.

"No, I won't! Hones' to goodness I won't!" promised the Topsy Doll. "Some folks do say I's terrible mischievous but I can't help it. I growed up dat way, I reckon!"

With that Topsy bent over and pulled one of the ears of Tumbling Tom.

"Hey there! Stop it!" cried that toy, and he leaned over to tickle Topsy, but he leaned too far and down he fell.

"Ha! Ha! Ha!" laughed the black Doll. "Golly, I's mischievous; but mah black won't rub off! Look!"

Topsy took up from the shelf a piece of the white paper Mr. Mugg used to wrap up the toys when they were purchased. Topsy rubbed this piece of paper on her black, shiny cheek as hard as she could rub it. Then she held it out to the China Cat. The paper was as white as before.

"See!" cried Topsy. "Mah black won't rub off! Now can't I play tag wif yo' all?"

"Oh, yes, let her; do!" begged the Talking Doll. "She's so cute!"

"Of course she may play if she will not smut me," said the China Cat. "Please don't believe I'm fussy," she went on; "but I shall never be sold if I do not keep myself white and clean. I thought at first that Topsy had been down in the coal bin."

"No'm," answered that colored Doll. "I's awful mischievous, but I don't play in no coal. No indeedy!"

"I'm glad of that," said the China Cat. "Now I'll be it, and see if I can tag any of you. Look out! I'm coming!"

With that the white Cat began chasing about on the shelves, trying to tag the other toys, who, you may be sure, kept well out of her reach.

"No fair tagging with your tail—that is so long!" called the Talking Doll, as she dodged around the corner of the Jack in the Box, who could not get loose to join the fun. "You must tag us with your paws."

"Yes, I'll do that," agreed the China Cat. "I'll only tag you with my paws. And I think I'll tag you right now!" she called to the Topsy Doll.

"Oh, ho! Yo' all here has got to be mighty lively to tag me!" the black toy laughed, and, just as the China Cat was about to touch her, Topsy dodged to one side and the China Cat nearly slipped off the shelf.

"Oh, my dear! you must be careful," cried the Talking Doll. "Think what would happen if you hit the floor!"

"Oh, I don't dare think of it!" mewed the China Cat, with a shudder. "I should be broken to bits!"

So after that the Cat did not run quite so fast. Topsy was a very lively little doll. She skipped here and there, and kept the other toys laughing at her funny tricks and the queer way her kinky hair bobbed about her head.

So the game went on, and at last the China Cat managed to touch the Jumping Jack with her paw.

"Tag! You're it!" cried the China Cat. "Now it's your turn to do the chasing, Mr. Jack!"

The game went on faster than ever, and such jolly fun as there was you never would have dreamed could happen in a toy shop, unless you could have seen it yourself. But of course that is not allowed. If you had so much as peeked in with one eye, all the toys would have become as quiet as a chocolate mouse.

At last they grew tired of such exciting fun. One after another had taken a turn at being it for tag.

"I know what let's do," suggested the Soldier Captain, after they had rested. "Let's have some riddles."

"Hi!" cried Topsy, "am riddles good to eat?"

"No, indeed," answered the Talking Doll. "Riddles are something you have to guess."

"Den I mus' be a riddle!" said the colored Doll.

"What makes you think so?" asked the China Cat.

"'Cause some ob de toys in mah pa't of de store says as how I kept 'em guessin'," was the answer. "Dey done say dey nebber know whut I'm gwine to do nex'. I suah mus' be a riddle."

"Oh, no, that isn't a riddle," the Soldier Captain explained. "A riddle is like a puzzle. For instance, I ask you what has four legs, and yet can't walk?"

"Hu! Dey ain't nothin' whut has fo' legs an' can't walk!" declared Topsy. "Dat's silly! I's got only two legs, but I can walk when nobody looks at me. An' dat Noah's Ark Elephant, he's got fo' legs, an' he can walk. What is dat has fo' legs an' can't walk I axes yo', Mr. Soldier Captain?"

"A table has four legs and yet it can't walk," laughed the wooden officer. "That's a riddle, Topsy. Now see if you can tell one."

So the Topsy Doll and the other toys began to think of riddles, asking them of one another. But, somehow or other, the China Cat was very still and quiet. She did not enter into this fun as she had into the game of tag.

"What's the matter?" asked the Jumping Jack, when he had guessed a funny riddle about a little green hen. "Are you watching for mice, China Cat? There are some little ones, made of cloth and wood over in the novelty department where Topsy came from."

"No, I am not thinking of mice," answered the China Cat. "To tell you the truth, Mr. Jumping Jack, I was thinking of the Nodding Donkey. He came back here, you know, to have his leg fixed, and he spoke about how happy he was with the little lame boy, who, I'm glad to know, is lame no longer. I was just wondering if I would go to a nice home such as he has."

"I suppose all us toys will be sold, one after another," said the Jumping Jack. "But it is so nice here that I dread to think of going away."

"Yes, it is nice in Mr. Mugg's store," the China Cat agreed. "But I suppose we must do as we are told. Dear Nodding Donkey! How I should like to see him again. I wonder—"

"Hush! Quiet, everybody! Back to your shelves!" suddenly cried Tumbling Tom. "Morning is about to come and Mr. Mugg and his daughters will soon be here. They must never catch us moving about!"

Such a scramble as there was! The China Cat, the Talking Doll, the Trumpeter, the Policeman, the Fireman, the Jumping Jack, Tumbling Tom and Jack Box all made haste to get on the shelves where they belonged.

The Topsy Doll, with her kinky hair, darted toward the novelty department.

"I's glad yo' all let me play wif yo'," she said in her queer talk. "An' I didn't get any black on yo'; did I, Miss China Cat?"

"No, indeed. You were very nice," was the answer. "Come and play with us again."

Then it was time for the toys to be very still and quiet, for the door of the store opened, and in came Mr. Mugg.

"Ah, this is going to be a lovely day!" said the jolly toy-shop man. "I shall do a good business to-day!"

A little later in came his daughters, Geraldine and Angelina. They began dusting and setting the store to rights for the day's business.

"Oh, my dear! look at this," said Angelina to her sister.

"What is the matter?" asked Geraldine, pausing with a feather duster under her arm.

"Why, the lovely white China Cat has a speck of dirt on her back," said Angelina. "I must have forgotten to dust her yesterday."

"Oh, my!" thought the China Cat, who heard what was said, though she could not turn around to lick off the speck with her red tongue, "some black must have come off Topsy after all."

"Oh, no, it isn't dirt," said Angelina, as she took the Cat down to look more closely at her. "It's just a little speck of black feather from my duster. It must have just got on."

"Oh, I'm so glad of that!" thought the white Cat. "I wouldn't want to think that Topsy's black rubbed off."

Soon the store was in readiness for customers, and among the first to enter that morning was a little girl. She was with a lady, who was the little girl's aunt.

"Now, Jennie," said the aunt, as Mr. Mugg came forward to wait on them, "what present would you like? You may pick out anything you please."

"Oh, Aunt Clara! How lovely of you!" cried Jennie Moore, for that was her name. "Let me see now. What would I like best?"

While Jennie was looking along the shelves of toys her aunt said in a low tone to Mr. Mugg:

"Jennie has been such a good girl, helping her mother who was ill, that I promised her any toy she wished."

"That is very kind of you, I am sure," said Mr. Mugg, rubbing his hands and looking over the tops of his glasses. "We have many toys here for good little girls, and for good boys, too. Not long ago I sold a Nodding Donkey to a lame boy, and, would you believe me; that boy isn't lame at all now," and Mr. Mugg laughed, and Aunt Clara laughed also.

But Jennie was looking along the shelves of toys. The China Cat looked down, and when she saw what a nice little girl Jennie was, so neat and clean, the China Cat thought to herself:

"If I have to be taken away and belong to some child, I think I should like to go to Jennie's house. I'm sure she would be kind to me and love me, and I would love her."

Jennie seemed to be thinking the same thing about the China Cat, for suddenly she reached up and took down the white toy.

"Here, Aunt Clara, this is what I would like," said Jennie.

She walked toward her aunt and Mr. Mugg with the China Cat in her hand, but, just before she reached them, Jennie tripped over a velocipede on the floor, and seemed about to fall.

"Oh, Jennie, don't drop that China Cat, whatever you do!" cried her aunt.

CHAPTER III

"FIRE! FIRE!"

Had Jennie Moore stumbled and dropped the China Cat to the floor of the toy shop that would have been the end of this book. For if the Cat had fallen she surely would have been broken to bits. And, though Mr. Mugg might have been able to glue the pieces together again, the China Cat never would have been like herself, and there would be no story about her.

But, as it happened, there was a soft footstool just in front of the velocipede over which Jennie stumbled, and the little girl fell down on that, still holding the China Cat in her hands. Not once did Jennie let go of the toy she had taken off the shelf.

"Oh, my dear little girl! I hope you did not hurt yourself!" cried Mr. Horatio Mugg, as he sprang forward to raise Jennie from the footstool, across which she had fallen.

"And I hope she hasn't broken the China Cat!" exclaimed Aunt Clara.

"Well," replied Mr. Mugg, with a kind smile, "breaking the China Cat would not have been so bad. I could easily send to the workshop of Santa Claus and get another toy. But nice little girls, if they fall and hurt themselves, are not so easily mended. I am glad you are not hurt, my dear," he went on, as he helped Jennie to her feet.

"And I am glad the China Cat is not broken," said Aunt Clara. "It is a lovely piece of work."

"Yes, it is one of my choicest toys," said Mr. Mugg. "It can not talk, like some of my dolls, nor spring about like some of the Jumping Jacks. But the Cat is so clean and white that it would be an ornament in any home."

"She'll look lovely on my bureau," said Jennie. "Does her head come off, Mr. Mugg?" the nice little girl asked, as her aunt was looking carefully at the China Cat.

"Oh, my, no!" laughed the toy-shop man. "I once had a cat whose head could be lifted off, and burned matches could be dropped down inside her. But this Cat isn't that kind."

"I should hope not!" thought the China Cat, while Aunt Clara was looking her over. "Not that I don't consider my cousin, the Match Cat, as nice as I am," she told herself, "but I'm just different; that's all! I hope I may go to live with this little girl. I shall be able to keep myself spotless and white in her home, I'm sure."

But the China Cat was not yet to leave the toy store. And there were some strange adventures soon to happen, as I shall tell you.

"Well, Jennie," said Aunt Clara, as she again let the little girl take the China Cat, "if you think you want this toy you may have it. But we will not take it with us now. I have some other shopping to do, and if we carry the Cat with us something may happen to her."

"Oh, can't I take her now?" pleaded Jennie.

"No, my dear," her aunt answered. "Mr. Mugg will put her aside for you, and I will come in to-morrow and get her."

"Yes, I'll save the China Cat for you," promised the toy man.

"If I may be sure of having her I don't mind," said Jennie. "But we must be sure and come after her to-morrow, Auntie."

"We will come to-morrow surely," said Aunt Clara, and then, after Jennie had taken one more look at the toy she hoped soon would be hers, she followed her aunt out of the store.

Mr. Mugg and his two daughters were very busy in their toy shop that day. A load of packing boxes arrived, direct from the North Pole workshop of Santa Claus, and these boxes were stored down in the basement.

"We will open those boxes some day next week," said Mr. Mugg to his daughters. "Perhaps among the new toys there may be another China Cat. I certainly hope so, for when Jennie's aunt comes for this one we shall feel lonesome."

Mr. Mugg took a box of matches and went down into the basement to light the gas and see about storing away the cases of new toys. And when the men had opened some, not taking many of the toys out, however, the storekeeper was called up stairs by one of his daughters.

"Leave the cases the way they are," he said to the expressmen. "Don't open any more. I'll do that later in the week."

Then Mr. Mugg turned the gas down low, for he thought he might come back again, and up the stairs he hurried to see what his daughter wanted. As he walked across the basement floor the box of matches dropped out of his pocket, near some straw from one of the packing cases.

"I'll get the matches when I come back," thought the toy man. But the rest of the day he was so busy he forgot all about them.

Back on the shelf, out of sight, the China Cat thought over what had happened that day.

"I surely am glad Jennie didn't let me fall and break," said the Cat to herself. "And I am glad I am going to belong to such a nice, clean little girl." Then, as one could see her, hidden away as she was, the China Cat washed her paws with her red tongue.

Once again night came. The toy store was closed, and all the lights turned out except a small one in the middle of the store. For a time it was quiet, and then, once more, the Trumpeter blew a jolly blast on his horn.

Toot! Toot! Toot! went the trumpet.

"Are you ready for more fun?" asked the Talking Doll.

"Yes," was the answer. "It is now night, no one can see us, and we can do as we please. Let's play tag again," said a number of toys.

"Where is the China Cat?" asked Tumbling Tom. "We don't want to leave her out of the good times."

"Oh, I'm here!" mewed the white pussy. "I'm just sort of hidden away so I will not be sold. I am to go to a little girl named Jennie Moore."

"Hum! Jennie Moore! Seems to me I heard her spoken of by the father of the little lame boy when the Nodding Donkey was brought back here to have his leg mended," said the Jumping Jack. "Wouldn't it be funny, Miss China Cat, if you should go to live in a house near your friend, the Nodding Donkey?"

"It would be very nice, I think," said the China Cat. "But I have something new to suggest," she went on, as she moved out near the edge of the shelf. "Instead of playing tag, why can't all of us go down into the basement?"

"What for?" asked Tumbling Tom.

"I heard it said that a new lot of toys was put down in the basement to-day," went on the China Cat. "Let's go down and call on them. It's always polite to call on new neighbors, you know," she added.

"Yes, let's do that!" shouted the Trumpeter. "We'll make them feel at home."

So down the cellar stairs trooped the China Cat, the Talking Doll, the Jumping Jack, Jack Box and many other toys.

Clip! Clap! Clump! they went down the stairs.

"Hello, new toys!" mewed the China Cat. "We have come to call on you!"

"That is very kind of you," said a Red Fireman, who was one of the new toys that had been taken from the boxes. "We were just wondering what sort of place this was—so dark and gloomy."

"Oh, this is the basement," said the China Cat. "The toy store is up above. You'll be brought up there with us, soon, we hope. But we came to visit you and cheer you up."

"And we are very glad," said a Cloth Doll. "I was getting tired of lying here on my back."

"Let us play some games," proposed the China Cat. "We can ask riddles, have a game of tag, or, those of you who are unpacked, can join in a race."

"I say let's have a race!" cried the Engineer of a toy train of cars on the floor. "I haven't had a race with my engine and cars since Mr. Mugg lifted us out of our box. Come on! I'll get up steam and have a race."

Before any one could stop him, the Engineer started his train of iron cars over the floor of the basement.

Toot! Toot! he blew the whistle.

Suddenly there was a crackling sound and then a flash of flame.

"What's the matter!" cried the China Cat.

"Oh, I have run over a box of matches!" exclaimed the toy Engineer. "They have begun to blaze and the straw from the packing cases is catching! Oh, look what I did, but I didn't mean to!"

Surely enough, the toy cars had run over the box of matches Mr. Mugg had dropped, and now the flames and smoke were filling the basement of the toy shop.

"Fire! Fire! Fire!" cried the toy Policeman, banging with his club.

CHAPTER IV

A LITTLE BLACK BOY

So many things began happening at once in the basement of the toy shop, after the train of cars ran over the box of matches, that the China Cat, the Jumping Jack and even the Policeman, who was supposed to keep order, never knew half that took place. All the toys knew was that they began to choke with the smoke from the burning straw, and some of them, who were too close to the box of blazing matches, felt the heat very much.

"We Must Hurry Out!" Mewed the China Cat. "We Must Hurry Out!" Mewed the China Cat.

"Oh, we must hurry out of here!" mewed the China Cat.

"I should say so!" exclaimed the Policeman. "Come on! Move lively! No loitering!" he cried, as he had done that time when he tickled the Nodding Donkey in the ribs with the club. "Everybody get out of the way of the fire!" went on the toy Policeman, swinging his club. "Where are the engines and the firemen?" he called.

"Here we are! I'm coming," cried an excited voice, and there clattered along the basement floor of the toy shop a little fire engine, on which was perched a toy Fireman.

"Let me get at the blaze!" cried this Fireman, who was dressed all in red. "Who started it, anyhow?"

"I did," answered the Engineer of the train of iron cars. "I ran over a box of matches, but I did not mean to."

"Well, it is going to be a bad fire!" said the Fireman. "Everybody must get out."

"Except you and me," added the Policeman, "I have ordered them all back to their shelves, but you and I must stay here. I will remain on guard while you put out the fire!" he said.

"Right!" cried the brave Fireman, as he got down off his engine.

By this time the straw had set fire to some of the wooden boxes which Mr. Mugg had opened that day to take out the toys. The burning straw and wood made more smoke than ever, so that the China Cat choked, and the Talking Doll was coughing so hard she could not speak.

"Hurry with that water!" ordered the Policeman. "Squirt a lot of water from the hose on the blaze, Mr. Fireman!"

But the sad part of it was that there was no water in the toy engine. They are not made that way, though sometimes boys, who get engines for presents, put water in them to play with. But though the Fireman ran out his tiny hose, and pointed it straight at the blaze, no water spurted from the nozzle.

"It is getting too hot here for me!" cried the Policeman. "I'm afraid we can't do anything, Mr. Fireman. We had better run upstairs with the rest of the toys!"

"What about the toys still in the boxes—those that Mr. Mugg has not unpacked?" asked the Fireman. "The toys still in the boxes can not get out to run upstairs."

"No, that's so," admitted the Policeman, stepping back out of the smoke, and scratching his nose with his club. "What shall we do?"

"I'll get my ax and chop open the boxes," the toy Fireman answered. "We fire-fighters have to do that. If only I had water in my engine I could soon put out this blaze."

But there was no use wishing that now, and, just as the Fireman had said, the poor toys, still nailed up in the boxes, were likely to have a hard time.

"Let us out! Please let us out!" begged the Dolls, the toy Dogs, the toy Cats and the other playthings, all shut up as they were. They could smell the smoke, if they could not see the blaze.

"I'll save you! The Policeman and I will get you out!" cried the brave Fireman, as he dashed back to his engine to get the small ax which hung there.

Meanwhile the China Cat, the Talking Doll and some of the Jumping Jacks were hurrying up the basement steps much faster than they had gone down. They wanted to get out of the fire and smoke.

"If only the Nodding Donkey were here, I'm sure he could have ridden me on his back out of danger," thought the China Cat. "He was very fond of me, and I like him. But he is not here!"

There was such a crowd of toys, all trying to get up the basement stairs at once, and the smoke was so thick now, that the Policeman and Fireman had also to run back, and there might have been a sad accident, only that the regular fire department men came along just then.

Some one in the street had seen smoke coming from the basement of the toy shop.

"Fire! Fire! Fire!" was the cry, and this time it was a real shout, and not such as the toys had given. Then the man who had smelled and seen the smoke ran and pulled an alarm box.

There was a clang of bells and loud toots of a whistle. There was a rush of many feet, and then a loud crash as the real firemen burst open the door of the toy shop.

"The fire is in the basement!" cried one fireman, wearing a rubber coat and hat to keep himself dry for the water would soon be spraying from the hose of the real, big engine.

"Yes, it's in the basement," said a real policeman, who had arrived almost as soon as had the firemen. "And Mr. Mugg has a lot of new toys down there. We must carry them out for him!"

Of course as soon as the door of the shop had been burst open, and the real firemen and policemen had come in, not a toy dared move or speak, for they would have been seen.

So they had to stay just where they were. Some were half way up the basement stairs; the China Cat had just reached the middle of the first floor, when she had to come to a stop; the Talking Doll was on the top step of the stairs, and there she had to stay. It was there that a fireman saw her as he was about to rush down into the basement. The firemen carried lanterns so they could see in the darkened store.

"The toys are scattered all about," said the fireman, picking up the Talking Doll. "There must have been an explosion!" Of course he did not know that the toys themselves had gone down into the basement to play, and that the fire was caused by the train running over the box of matches.

"We must carry out some of these toys before we begin to squirt the water, or they will all be spoiled," said the fireman who had picked up the Talking Doll. "Water will ruin them as much as the blaze. Come on, boys!" he called. "Save the toys!"

Here and there about the store, and down in the basement, rushed the firemen and policemen. Toys that were scattered about were hastily piled in open boxes. Then the boxes were dragged out on the sidewalk. Quite a crowd gathered in the street, for more engines, firemen and policemen were arriving all the while.

"Oh, this is dreadful!" thought the China Cat, as a whiff of smoke blew in her face. "I shall be all blackened and ruined!"

Clang! Clang! rang the bells on the real fire engine. Toot! Toot! blew the whistles.

"Here is a toy cat! Put her in that box!" called one fireman to another, who was dragging out a wooden box into which he had tossed the Talking Doll, a

Jumping Jack and a dozen Green Pigs. "Take them out; and then we must begin to use the water! The fire is getting too hot!"

The China Cat could feel the heat, and she noticed that the red color on the cheeks of a Painted Doll was all running down, making her look very streaked.

"Oh, what a bump!" thought the China Cat, as she felt herself tossed into the packing box. She landed in between the Talking Doll and a Jumping Jack.

"Out on the sidewalk with that box!" cried the fireman, and he and some others began dragging out the one in which was the China Cat.

There had been a great deal of noise and excitement in the store, but there was five times as much noise out on the sidewalk. Just as the box containing the China Cat was dragged toward the door, a shower of water sprinkled down.

"Oh, dear me!" thought the China Cat. "I can't bear to be wet, and now it is raining! But I hope it will wash from me some of the black smoke."

However, it was not rain that the China Cat felt, but water from the hose of a real engine. The firemen were beginning to squirt water on the blaze, to save as much as they could of Mr. Mugg's store and of his toys, and some of the water from the hose sprayed on the China Cat.

By this time it was getting to be morning, and crowds of men and boys, with a few women, on their way to early work, stopped to look at the fire. Smoke was pouring out of Mr. Mugg's basement, and some one had hurried to the toy-shopkeeper's house to awaken him and his daughters and tell them what was happening.

"Oh, look at the toys!" cried a group of boys, as they came running up the street to see where the fire was. "Oh, look at 'em!"

"Keep back now! Let those toys alone!" warned a policeman who was on guard.

Most of the boys stepped back off the sidewalk, but when the policeman's back was turned a little black boy, who stood somewhat apart from the others, sneaked up to the packing box into which the China Cat and the Talking Doll had been thrown.

"Golly, what a lot ob toys!" murmured the little negro boy, whose name was Jeff. "I reckon as how I kin git one fo' nuffin, if dat p'liceman don't see me."

Jeff, who was dirty and ragged, watched his chance. He had come from his home in a tenement house, not far from the fire, and his eyes glistened when he saw so many toys out on the street.

"Um-ah! Jest look at 'em!" murmured Jeff. "Golly! I kin git one as easy as not outen dat open box! Wait till dat p'liceman turns around."

Jeff watched his chance. The policeman on guard moved off to one side. In an instant Jeff, the dirty little black boy, sneaked up, and, thrusting in his hand, which was black with dirt as well as being covered with black skin, he took up the pure, white China Cat.

"Dis am just whut I want!" whispered Jeff.

"Oh, my, how dirty he is! Oh, I can't bear to have him touch me!" thought the China Cat. "I dread dirt more than I do water! Oh, what shall I do?"

But she had no chance to do anything just then, for, with a quick motion, Jeff, the colored boy, thrust the China Cat inside his dirty, ragged blouse.

"Oh, I'll be smothered!" thought the poor China Cat. "What a dreadful fate to be taken away by a dirty boy! And only an hour ago I was so happy! Oh, dear! Oh, dear! Oh, dear!"

CHAPTER V

ROUGH PLAY

You can just imagine how the China Cat felt. Always so clean and white, always washing herself if she found the least speck of dirt on her, always keeping as much as possible away from dust and grime—and now to be spattered with water, blackened by the smoke of the fire, and finally thrust inside the soiled blouse of a not very clean boy! Oh, it was terrible!

The China Cat said it was, over and over again; to herself, of course, for she dared not speak aloud, nor so much as mew, while Jeff, the colored boy, had her. And Jeff certainly had the China Cat.

Jeff's eyes sparkled with delight as he pressed the toy up under his blouse, out of sight, and then he darted away from the pile of toys, on the sidewalk—toys that had hastily been carried out of the burning store.

"Hi, golly! I's done gone fool dat p'liceman," murmured Jeff, as he stepped off the sidewalk and made his way out of the crowd in front of the burning store. "He tole me to keep away from dem toys! But I sneaks up when he isn't lookin', an' I gits de bestest toy ob all! Golly! I's smarter dan a p'liceman, I is!"

Jeff grinned, showing two rows of white teeth in his black face. Indeed, Jeff's teeth were the only clean things about him, it seemed. At least they were white, though I can not say that he ever used a tooth brush. His teeth were as white as was the China Cat when she was her very cleanest. But she was not at all clean now. And you know how unhappy this made her feel.

There was so much excitement now in front of Mr. Mugg's toy shop, with the fire, the smoke, the water, the fire engines, the firemen and the police, to say nothing of the crowd that had gathered, that no one paid any attention to Jeff. Away he sneaked, with the China Cat under his blouse.

"I's smart, I is!" said Jeff to himself, grinning. "I could 'a' tooken a lot ob toys; but I liked dis Cat bestest ob all. She's so white!"

Jeff did not mind the black specks from the fire that had settled on the cat, and he cared nothing about the grimy marks his own dirty hands had made.

It was broad daylight now, and the firemen were getting the best of the fire. By pouring a lot of water from their hose down in the basement, the blaze had been put out, though there was still much smoke.

Jeff, the negro boy, shuffled off down the street on his way back to his home. When he was nearly there he met some other colored boys.

One of these lads, named Sam, saw that Jeff was hiding something under his blouse.

"Hello, Jeff!" called Sam. "Whut yo' got there? Something good to eat?"

"Nope, 'tain't nuffin to eat!" declared Jeff. He and Sam talked negro talk, of course, just like Topsy, the colored doll, whom the China Cat at first thought would rub off some of her black.

"Whut yo' got then?" asked Sam. "Show me!"

"Yes, show what yo' got, Jeff!" cried the other colored boys.

"Oh, I ain't got nuffin much!" Jeff answered, as he moved away from Sam and the other boys. Sometimes they had taken things away from Jeff, and Jeff was afraid that was what they were now going to do. Inside the blouse of the colored boy the China Cat heard what was said, but she could see nothing.

"I wonder what is going to happen?" she thought.

"Jeff has got something!" declared Sam to his chums. "Let's catch him an' take it away!"

"All right!" agreed the other colored boys. They made a rush for Jeff, but he was too quick for them. Pressing his hands over his blouse, at the spot where the China Cat was stuffed, so she would not bounce out, Jeff ran down the street.

"I's got something yo' can't have!" he cried. "An' yo' all can't catch me, an' git it; dat's whut yo' can't!"

Away he sped, and he was such a good runner that the other boys could not come up to him. Around the corner of one street, down another and up a third ran Jeff, and then he darted down the stairs into what was almost a cellar, though it was called a basement. It was here, in some poor, miserable rooms, that Jeff lived with his brothers and sisters.

"Whut de mattah, Jeff?" asked his mother, a large, fat, colored washerwoman. "Am de p'licemans after yo' a'gin?"

Jeff had run so hard that he was out of breath, and could not speak for a few moments. Hidden as she was, inside his blouse, the China Cat could feel Jeff's heart pumping hard, and notice his rapid breathing.

"Dear me!" thought the China Cat, "this is a dreadful state of affairs. I wonder if I am ever to get out of this smothering place. I don't like it, cooped up like this! I want to get out in the air, and have Geraldine or Angelina wash me!"

You see the China Cat did not know all that had happened to her. She hoped she would soon be back in Mr. Mugg's store, washed nice and clean, and set on a shelf. But the store of poor Mr. Mugg was in a sad state now, even though the fire had been put out.

As Jeff's breathing became easier, his brothers and sisters, who were just getting up out of their beds, crowded around him. His mother, who was getting breakfast, asked him again:

"Jeff, am de p'licemans tryin' to git yo'?"

"Nope!" answered the colored boy. "I runned 'cause I wanted to git away from Sam Brown an' his crowd. Dey was gwine to take mah cat away from me!"

"Yo' cat?" cried Jeff's mother. "Where'd yo' git a cat?"

Jeff wiggled and twisted as he reached his hand inside his blouse and pulled out the China Cat.

"Dere she am!" he cried, holding her up. "Dere's mah pussy! I done got her at de fire, an' de p'liceman didn't see me!"

For a moment there was silence in the dingy basement tenement where Jeff lived. His brothers and sisters, all smaller than he, crowded up around him as he held the China Cat high in the air.

"Ain't she jess boo'ful!" murmured one little black girl.

"Kin she wiggle her haid, like I done see a Donkey shake his haid in de toy shop?" asked one of Jeff's brothers.

"Lemme hab her!" pleaded the littlest black girl of all.

"No, suh!" declared Jeff. "Dis am mah white pussy, dat I done took outen de fire an' de p'liceman didn't see me, an' I's gwine to keep her, I is!"

He held the China Cat higher above his head.

"Oh, mercy me!" thought the poor white pussy, "I hope he doesn't let me fall. Oh, how miserable I am! So dirty, and in such an unpleasant place! I thought I'd be back in the toy shop with the Talking Doll and my other friends!"

The China Cat did not at first know where she was when Jeff pulled her out from beneath his blouse. It had been dark in there, but it was lighter in the kitchen, and this confused the toy animal. But when she had a chance to look around, held up high in the air as she was, she did not at all like her new home. And she was very much afraid that Jeff would let her fall.

But the colored boy did not. He set the China Cat on the table, right down in a little puddle of molasses that had been spilled when the table was set for breakfast.

"Oh, dear me, this is worse and worse!" thought the China Cat, as she felt the sticky stuff on her tail. "I shall never get clean and white again now!"

As for Jeff and his brothers and sisters, they did not seem to mind a bit of molasses on the table. Indeed, one of the little colored girls put her finger in the sweet, sticky puddle, and then she put her finger in her mouth.

"Dat's good!" she murmured. "Me 'ikes 'lasses, me does!"

But the others were more interested in the China Cat. They stared at her with all their eyes, and Jeff's mother asked:

"Where yo' done say yo' got her?"

"At de fire," Jeff explained. "I heard de engines puffin' past early dis mawnin', an' I gits up an' goes out. Dere was a toy store on fire, an' dey frowed a lot ob toys out in de street. Dere was Jumpin' Jacks, an' Dolls, an' Steamboats, an'—an'—"

Two of the older colored boys started on a rush for the door, one of them crying:

"I'se gwine to git a steamboat!"

"Yo' can't git none now, Sim!" shouted Jeff. "De p'licemans is all aroun' de place. Dey won't let you take nuffin. But I done fooled 'em. Anyhow, de fire's out now, an' dey'll be puttin' de toys back. But I done got a white cat!"

So he had, but the China Cat was not so very white now. Besides the dirt from the fire and the grime from Jeff's hands, she was sticky with molasses, and every bit of dust flying about the basement room seemed to settle on the poor toy pussy.

"Lemme hab her, Jeff!" pleaded one of his sisters.

"Well, I done let yo' hold her for a minute," said Jeff, and he gave the China Cat into the hands of the little black girl. But as this girl had been eating bread and sugar, she got the poor China Cat stickier than ever.

"Lemme hold her now, Jeff!" pleaded another black tot.

"Nope, I ain't held her long 'nuff!" declared the first.

"Heah! Gib her to me!" ordered the second.

"No! No! Jeff said I could hab her!" cried the first.

One tried to take the China Cat away from the other, and in the scramble a chair was upset and the toy nearly fell to the floor.

"This is the most dreadful place I was ever in!" thought the China Cat, who, of course, could do nothing to save herself. "If they let me fall I shall be broken, all dirty and soiled as I am."

But Jeff was not going to let that happen.

"Heah! Gib me back mah cat, whut I done got at de fire!" he said, and he grabbed it from his sister's hand.

"Oh! Oh! Oh!" wailed the little black girl.

"Heah! Hush yo' noise now!" called Jeff's mother. "Set up to de table an' hab yo' brekfus'! Stop playin'!"

"Dear me, they call that playing!" thought the China Cat. "I wonder what they would do in a game of tag? Oh, what is ever to become of me?"

Jeff took the toy and set it on a shelf in the kitchen, and then he sat down to his breakfast. Every once in a while he would look up at the China Cat.

"I's glad I done got yo'," Jeff would murmur. "Yo' suah am a fine toy!"

After breakfast he took the China Cat down off the shelf and let his sisters look at her. But no sooner did one of the little colored girls have the cat in her hands than she darted out of the basement.

"Now I's got her, an' I's gwine t' hab some fun!" cried Arabella. Arabella was the name of this one of Jeff's sisters. "I's gwine to hab fun wid dis cat!"

Up the stairs and out into the street she ran, holding the China Cat in such a tight grip that, had the toy been a real pussy, she would have been choked.

CHAPTER VI

A TERRIBLE STORM

Jeff was not going to let his China Cat be taken from him in this fashion. With a yell he darted up the basement steps and ran after his sister.

"Come back heah! Bring back mah cat!" yelled the colored boy.

"No! No!" screamed his sister. "I done got her, an' she's mine now! She suah is mine!"

Faster and faster the little colored girl raced down the street, but of course she could not run as fast as Jeff, who soon caught up to her. Reaching forth his hands, which were now dirtier than before, Jeff caught hold of his sister's kinky hair.

"Ouch! Oh, yo' stop dat, Jeff!" she wailed.

"Gib me back mah white cat!" he demanded, and he took the toy roughly from his sister. Arabella began to cry, and a man who was passing stopped and looked at the colored children.

"What are you doing?" he asked.

"Oh, we's only playin'," answered Jeff. "She took mah cat, an' I wanted it back."

"Hum!" mused the man. "That's a queer kind of play, I think. And if you drop that cat on the sidewalk you won't be able to play with her, for she'll be broken to pieces."

"What a dreadful thing! Oh, if that should happen!" thought the China Cat, who heard all that was said.

"I ain't gwine to drop her," declared Jeff, as he turned away with the China Cat in his dirty hands. With tears on her black cheeks, Arabella followed her brother back to the tenement.

Jeff put his toy down on the table again. On one wall of the room was a looking glass. It was cracked and not very clean, but as a ray of sunshine entered the dingy basement the China Cat, by the gleam of it, saw her reflection.

"Why, I hardly know myself!" she whispered, not daring, of course, to speak aloud or to move and make believe come to life. There were too many colored children looking at her. "Oh, what a fright I am!" thought the China Cat and sighed.

Well might she think that. On her nose was a big speck of dirt, and there were other specks on her back and sides. Her tail, too, that was always so spotless, was now daubed with molasses and smoke grime from the fire. The China Cat was white now only in spots.

"The Nodding Donkey would hardly speak to me if he saw me now," she thought. "I'm glad he isn't here."

"Now don't yo' touch my cat!" warned Jeff, as he got up from the table, where he had been playing with the toy.

"Whut yo' gwine do?" asked Arabella, who had got over her crying spell.

"I's gwine make a stable fo' my cat," answered the colored lad.

"Cat's don't live in stables! Dey lives in under de back porch," said Arabella. "In a box."

"Cats do so live in stables, 'cause I done seen 'em!" declared Jeff. "An' dey catches rats an' mice. I's gwine make a stable fo' my cat whut I done got at de fire an' de p'liceman didn't see me!" and he laughed as he thought of how he had fooled the officer.

Jeff hunted around in the woodpile until he found what he wanted. This was a large cigar box, and with a knife Jeff soon cut a hole in one side, large enough to slip the China Cat through.

"Dere's her stable!" he declared with satisfaction.

As for the China Cat, when she was shut up in the cigar box, she wanted, most dreadfully, to sneeze. For the box smelled very strongly of tobacco, and it made her nose tickle. But she dared not so much as utter a faint aker-choo for fear she would be heard. So the China Cat held back the sneeze, though it made her nose ache, and she was very glad when Jeff took her out of the cigar box stable.

During the remainder of that day the colored boy and his sisters and brothers took turns playing with the China Cat. For, after a while, Jeff allowed the others to handle his toy. And the China Cat was passed around among the colored children so often that she kept getting more and more dirty. And on account of having spots of molasses on her, every bit of dirt and grime that touched her stuck right there. Jeff and his brothers and sisters did not think of washing themselves, much less of washing the China Cat.

At last, after having been much handled and passed from one to another, the China Cat was set on a shelf in the kitchen of the basement tenement where the colored family lived. Many other colored folk lived in the same house, and in adjoining houses.

"At last I have time to breathe, but I am so dirty I do not know what to do," said the China Cat to herself. "I do not believe that any of the other toys that came from the workshop of Santa Claus ever had such an unpleasant adventure as I am having."

But if the China Cat had only known it, the Lamb on Wheels, about whom one of these Make Believe books has been written, had an adventure almost as sad. The Lamb went down into a coal bin, which was a great deal blacker than the negro tenement.

"I wonder what will happen to me next?" thought the China Cat, as she found herself perched on the kitchen shelf. She could look down and see Jeff, his brothers and his sisters, and his father and mother, eating supper. They did not offer the China Cat anything to eat, of course. Toys don't have to eat, which is very lucky sometimes.

"Come now, chilluns! Off to bed wif yo' all!" called Jeff's mother, when supper was finished. "Yo' was up early, an' yo' mus' git to bed early."

"Can't I play with my China Cat?" asked Jeff.

"No, indeedy!" declared the colored woman, shaking her head. "Yo' leave dat cat alone, an' git to bed!"

So to bed went Jeff and the other children. Their beds were down in the basement, in a room just off the kitchen. It was not a very nice home, but it was the best they could get.

Soon it began to grow dark, but there was a street lamp that shone in one of the basement windows, so the China Cat, who could see pretty well in the dark anyhow, managed to look about her.

On the same shelf where she sat, and not far away, was a little Cloth Dog.

"Dear me!" said the China Cat, speaking out loud now, for there was no one in the kitchen, all the family having gone to bed. "Dear me, I didn't know you were here!"

"Oh, yes, I'm here!" barked the Cloth Dog. "That is, what's left of me."

He and the China Cat did not quarrel, though in real life very few dogs and cats are friends. But it is much different with toys.

"Why, has anything happened to you?" asked the China Cat.

"Gracious, yes!" exclaimed the Cloth Dog. "Can't you see that my tail is pulled off?"

The China Cat stretched her neck and looked at the Cloth Dog. Surely enough, in the gleam from the street light she saw that he had no tail.

"Oh, how dreadful!" mewed the Cat. "How did it happen? It must pain you?"

"Not so much as at first," said the Dog. "I'm used to it now. One of the colored children pulled my tail off. I think it was the one they call Arabella. She's always grabbing things away from the others."

"Yes, she grabbed me," said the China Cat. "But I'm glad she didn't pull off my tail. I'm dirty and sticky, and I hardly know myself, but, thank goodness, I'm all here."

"That's more than I can say of myself," said the Cloth Dog sadly. "And I'm afraid you will not be all there after a few days in this house. It's a dreadful place, and the children are so rough!"

"How did you come to be here?" asked the China Cat. "Were you brought here from the workshop of Santa Claus?"

"Bless your whiskers, no!" barked the Cloth Dog. "Of course I once came from North Pole Land, but that was years ago. I was a good-looking toy then, and I had a fine tail. But after a while the children with whom I lived grew tired of me. I was tossed about, thrown into corners, and at last put out in the ashes. There one of these colored children found me, and brought me here. And the very first day there was a scrabble and a fight over me, and my tail was pulled off."

"Oh, I'm so sorry to hear that!" sighed the China Cat. "If you could only be taken to the store of Mr. Mugg he would put a new tail on you. He mended the broken leg of the Nodding Donkey."

"I'm afraid it is too late," whined the Cloth Dog. "But I am sorry for you. You are such a fine toy, and almost new."

"Yes, I am quite new. In fact, I have never been sold as yet," said the Cat. "I wouldn't be out of the store now, except for the fire. I was going to be taken by a very nice little girl named Jennie Moore. But now, alas, it is too late for that!"

"Tell me about the fire," begged the Cloth Dog. "It will make me forget that I have no tail."

So there on the shelf in the tenement kitchen, the China Cat told the Cloth Dog the story of the fire in the toy shop, and how she had come to be taken away by Jeff.

"I wondered where he had found you when I saw him bring you in this morning," barked the Dog, when the Cat finished her story. "Indeed, you have had many adventures; almost as many as I."

The two unfortunate toys became very friendly there in the half darkness of the night. The Cat was just telling about the Nodding Donkey, and how he had made the lame boy smile, when she suddenly stopped mewing.

"What's the matter?" asked the Cloth Dog.

"I heard a noise," said the China Cat.

"Oh, that's only rain," went on the Dog. "It is raining hard outside, and you hear it more plainly here because we are so near the street. Don't worry. Though this place is dirty, no rain comes in."

So the Cat went on with her story, but as the rain came down harder and faster it brought her another adventure.

Not far from the tenement was a river. And because there had been much rain before this last hard shower, the river had risen very high, until it was almost ready to overflow the banks.

Down pelted the rain, and soon there was a louder roar in the street outside.

"Is that just the rain?" asked the Cat of the Dog.

"It does sound a little different," the Dog replied. "I wonder if anything is happening? And see, what is that on the floor?"

"It is water!" cried the Cat, catching the gleam of it in the light of the street lamp. "Water is running in under the door!" she added.

"Then the river must be overflowing," barked the Dog. "The water is running in here. Oh, what shall we do?"

As the two toys watched they saw the puddle of water on the floor grow larger. The rain pelted down harder than before, and all at once there was a shouting in the streets.

"Get out! Get out, everybody!" came the cry. "There's a big flood! The river is rising! Get up and get out, everybody!"

CHAPTER VII

THE RESCUE

For a few moments after this wild shouting in the street there was no sound in the negro basement where the China Cat and the Cloth Dog without any tail were perched on the shelf. The rain pelted down harder than before, a regular flood in itself, and to the noise of the drops was added the roar from the flooded river.

Presently there came a pounding on the basement door of the tenement where Jeff, the colored boy, lived.

Bang! Bang! Bang! came the loud knock.

"Who's dat?" asked Jeff's mother from the bedroom where she was sleeping. "Who's dat knockin' at de do'?"

Bang! Bang! Bang! came the sound again.

"Can that be thunder?" whispered the China Cat to the Cloth Dog.

"No, this isn't a thunderstorm," answered the Dog. "It is much worse than any thunderstorm I ever heard. There is going to be a bad time here, with a flood and everything."

"Who's dat?" asked the voice of Jeff's mother again, as the pounding at the door sounded a second time.

"The police!" was the answer.

Jeff, who had been awakened, heard this answer. He covered his head with the clothes, and cowered down in the bed.

"Oh, mah good land!" thought Jeff when he heard this. "De p'lice has done come to git me 'cause I took de China Cat! Oh, good land! I ain't so smart as I thought! Oh, dey's gwine 'rest me suah!"

But the police had not come to get Jeff. Once more the officer pounded with his club on the basement door.

"Come there!" he cried. "Get up and dress and skip out if you don't want to be drowned! The river is rising. It will flood all these basement tenements! You'll have to clear out—all of you! Wake up and get out! We'll help you! Open the door!"

"Oh, massy me! A flood!" cried Jeff's mother. "Does yo' heah dat, Rastus?" she called to her husband. "Dere's a flood an' we's done got to run out! Git up an' open de do' an' I'll roust up de chilluns!"

"I'll open the do,' Ma," said Jeff, slipping out of his bed, and as he swung the door open there stood a policeman.

"Come, boy; lively!" cried the officer. "You were long enough answering my knock. You've all got to leave here! How many of you are there?"

"Ten," answered Jeff, and he looked over the mantel shelf to see if the officer noticed the China Cat.

But the policeman had something else to do just then. He and others had been sent to the tenement district, near the rising river, to rouse and save the poor people from the flood.

"Ten, eh?" cried the policeman. "That's quite a family. Well, don't stop to put on more than a few clothes. There isn't any time to save things. The river will be pouring in here soon."

"Some of it's heah already," remarked Jeff, as he saw the water on the floor.

"Lively now!" called the policeman again. "Here, let me take some of those," he said, as Jeff's father came out of a bedroom carrying in his arms two sleepy little colored girls.

The policeman wore a big rubber raincoat, which was dripping wet, and in the gleam of a light, which Jeff's father made, the wet rubber coat glistened brightly.

The policeman took the two little sisters of Jeff, and tucked them under his rubber coat. They were too sleepy to cry, having just been lifted from bed.

"This will keep you dry," said the officer. "I'll put you in the wagon and send you to the station house."

"Is yo'—is yo' gwine to 'rest 'em?" asked Jeff.

"Arrest 'em? No. What for?" asked the officer, with a smile, as he splashed, with his rubber boots, into the puddle of water on the tenement floor. "They haven't done anything, and you haven't done anything to be arrested for, have you?"

Jeff looked at the White China Cat, but did not answer.

"I'll just carry these youngsters out to the wagon, and then come back for more," the policeman went on. "You'll all be kept safe in the station house, or some place, until the river goes down."

Jeff breathed easier. He was afraid it had been found out that he took the China Cat. He darted quickly back into his bedroom and began putting on his shoes. That was all he had taken off when he curled up to go to sleep. He had only a few clothes, and he slept in them. So did most of the other children of the tenements in cold weather.

Out into the rain splashed the policeman carrying the two little colored girls. They were softly crying now, but he comforted them as best he could, and kept them dry under his coat. The rain was coming down harder than ever and the roar of the rising river was louder. When Jeff's father and mother and the other children were ready to be taken out, the water on the floor of the tenement was up to the policeman's knees.

"You'll have to hurry!" he called to the frightened family. "We have to rescue a lot of other people. Skip out and get into the wagon and you'll be safe."

As Jeff and the others made their way up the steps to the sidewalk they saw and heard more of the terrible storm. There was water in the streets. With the rising of the river and the rain, the streets were almost like little creeks themselves. Outside the tenement stood the police patrol wagon. As many of the poor people as possible had been crowded into it, Jeff and his folks among them.

"Are any more left in your rooms?" asked the officer who had pounded with his club on the door to awaken the sleepers.

"No, we's all out," answered Jeff's mother.

"Think I'll take a look and make sure," said the policeman. Back through the flood he waded in his rubber boots, and down he went into the basement where the lamp was still burning.

"Any one here?" asked the officer.

He listened, but there was no sound save the pelting of the rain, the roar of the river, and the trickle of water as it rose higher and higher in the basement. Up on their shelf the China Cat and the Cloth Dog sat and looked down. They had not dared to speak or move while any one was in the room. But they had just begun to feel that it was time for them to do something to save themselves when the policeman came in again. Then they had to remain quiet, though they were much afraid of being drowned in the flood.

"Hello!" suddenly exclaimed the police officer as he saw the China Cat. "Seems to me I know you! I remember about you! I wonder how you got here? You were among the toys taken from Mr. Mugg's shop during the fire. Well! Well! To think of finding you here, Miss China Cat! I shouldn't be surprised but what that oldest colored boy might know something about you. But I'll take you along, and hand you back to Mr. Mugg, where you belong."

With that the policeman reached up, lifted down the China Cat, and thrust her into an inside pocket, where his rubber coat would keep her nice and dry.

"Though if he only knew it," thought the China Cat, "I'd just as soon be rained on a little, to clean me off. Oh, but I am so dirty!"

However, the policeman did not stop to think that perhaps the Cat might like to be cleaned. In fact, he did not think she had any feelings at all, for it was a long while since he had been little enough to play with toys and enjoy make believe games.

Into his pocket went the China Cat. Then the policeman looked at the Cloth Dog on the shelf.

"You never came from the toy shop, that's certain," said the officer. "No use taking you!"

So he left the poor Cloth Dog, without any tail, alone on the kitchen shelf, but he took the China Cat away with him in his pocket, the policeman did.

Out into the rain-soaked street the officer made his way once more.

"Nobody left in here, Jim," he called to the other officer on the police wagon. "Get those people to the station, and then come back. There's a lot more who will have to be rescued this night. It's going to be a bad flood."

And so it was, though the China Cat saw little of it, for she was safe and snug in the officer's pocket. It was black and dark in there, but it was warm, though a bit smothery. And it was clean, which the China Cat liked best of all.

"Though I am very dirty myself," she said. "I hope I get somewhere so I can wash."

All night long the rescue of people from the flood was kept up. Jeff and his family were taken to a place of refuge where they were given something to eat and beds on which to lie down. All night long the policemen worked, and when morning came all those who had been in danger were saved.

The officer who had the China Cat in his pocket walked into his station house just as day was breaking.

"Here is something you'll like to hear about," said the policeman to the sergeant behind the desk, as he set the toy on the top of it.

"A cat! My land! where'd you get her?" asked the sergeant. "She'll be just what we want to catch mice around here! Here, puss, puss!" he called.

"Oh, my! he thinks I'm alive," said the China Cat to herself.

CHAPTER VIII

JENNIE GETS THE CAT

The policeman who had rescued the China Cat from the flood in the basement of the negro tenement stood and looked at the sergeant behind the desk in the station house. Then the policeman looked at the China Cat which he had set on top of the desk.

"What's the matter with you? Why are you acting so funny?" asked the sergeant of the policeman.

"Funny? I'm not acting funny. You are," the policeman laughed.

"How am I funny?" the sergeant wanted to know.

"Why, you're calling that cat, and asking her to catch mice, and—"

"Of course I'm asking her to catch mice," said the sergeant. "There's a lot of mice around here and—"

"Ha! Ha!" laughed the policeman. "That cat will never catch any mice. She's a toy, a China Cat, and she was stolen from that toy shop where there was a fire yesterday. It was Horatio Mugg's place. A lot of the toys were set out on the sidewalk, and some negroes who live near by walked off with quite a lot. Mr. Mugg, after the fire, made out a list of his toys that were missing, and among them was this China Cat. I had one of the lists.

"Then, when I was sent to rescue the people from the flood, I saw this Cat on the mantel. I brought her here, as I do with all stolen things I find, and you can send her back to Mr. Mugg."

The sergeant put on his glasses, for he was rather an elderly man, and looked carefully at the China Cat.

"Bless me!" exclaimed the sergeant, "she is a China Cat after all. I took her for a real black and white pussy."

"Oh, dear me!" thought the China Cat. "He thought I was partly black! I must be very dirty indeed. My toy friends would never know me! Oh, shall I ever be clean again?"

"Yes, it is only a toy China Cat," said the policeman who had rescued the pussy, as well as the negro family. "I guess she was pure white once. But she got blackened in the fire, and it didn't wash off in the flood, though goodness knows it rained enough!"

"I should say so," agreed the sergeant. "Well, leave the China Cat here, and I will send her back to Mr. Mugg. You didn't see any of his other stolen toys, did you?"

37

"No," the policeman answered, "I did not. There was a little Cloth Dog on the same shelf, but he had no tail and one eye was almost gone, so I knew he didn't belong in the toy store, and I let him stay there."

"Poor little Cloth Dog!" thought the China Cat. "I wonder what will become of him?"

However, she never heard, nor did she ever again see her little friend without any tail. But I might tell you that the little Cloth Dog was still on the mantel when the flood went down and Jeff and the family moved back into their basement. The Cloth Dog was not drowned, and he lived for many years after that, even without his tail, though I cannot say he was very happy.

"Well, you take care of the China Cat. I am going to get my breakfast," said the policeman who had brought the white pussy into the station house.

"I'll take care of her, and send her back to Mr. Mugg as soon as I have a chance," the sergeant promised.

Then he set the China Cat off the top of the big desk, and on a smaller one, so she would not get broken. All the remainder of the morning the China Cat was in the police station, though she was not arrested, you understand. Oh, my, no! She had done nothing wrong, even though she was very dirty. But of course being dirty was not her fault.

The China Cat saw many strange sights as she sat in the police station, and some of the sights were sad ones. She heard much about the flood, too, for it was a very high one, the river having overflowed its banks in many places.

At last all the poor people were rescued, and the police sergeant, who had been very busy, was given a few moments' rest. He leaned back in his chair and looked at the China Cat.

"I think I shall telephone Mr. Mugg and tell him to come here and get his China Cat," the sergeant said. "This may not be his toy. It may have been stolen from some other store. But I'll soon find out."

So the police sergeant telephoned to Mr. Mugg. The toy-store keeper and his daughters, Angelina and Geraldine, were very busy, getting things to rights after the fire. It had not been as bad as was at first supposed, being down in the basement. Some smoke and water got up on the main floor, however, but this was soon cleaned up and the store put to rights again.

"What's that?" cried Mr. Mugg over the telephone, though of course the China Cat could not hear what he said. "You have my white China Cat? Oh, I am so glad! I'll be right down to get her."

"All right," answered the sergeant. "She is here waiting for you. Though I would not call her very white," he added as he hung up the telephone.

"What do you think of that, Geraldine—Angelina!" called Mr. Mugg to his two daughters. "Our China Cat, that was stolen when the toys were carried out on account of the fire, has been found!"

"Oh, I am so glad!" said Geraldine.

"Where is she?" asked Angelina.

"In the police station," her father replied. "I am going down to get her."

"I'll go with you," offered Geraldine. "I want to see the China Cat again. I hope she isn't chipped. Who had her?"

But this Mr. Mugg did not know, for the sergeant did not tell him the whole story over the telephone. A little later Mr. Mugg and Geraldine were in the police station.

"I have come for my China Cat," said Mr. Mugg, rubbing his hands and looking over the tops of his glasses.

"Here she is," said the sergeant, and he handed over the pussy who had been rescued from the flood.

For a moment the toy-store keeper looked at the plaything. Then he sadly shook his head.

"No, I am sorry to say that is not my China Cat," he said.

Well, you can just imagine how the China Cat felt. Her heart, such as she had, was beating with joy when she saw Mr. Mugg and Geraldine come into the station house. But now to hear Mr. Mugg say she was not his Cat! Oh, it was terrible, I do assure you!

"Not your Cat?" exclaimed the sergeant. "Why, I understood a lot of toys were stolen from your shop after the fire, and a China Cat was among them."

"Yes, that is so," answered Mr. Mugg. "But my China Cat was a white one, and this is black and white. No, she does not belong to me."

He turned away, and the China Cat would have shed tears if China Cats ever cry. But Miss Geraldine stepped forward.

"Please let me look at that toy," she said.

The sergeant handed her the China Cat. Geraldine looked closely at her. Then she gave a joyful cry.

"Why, of course she is our Cat, Father!" said Geraldine. "She is just grimy and dirty. That's the reason you think she is black and white. If I could only wash her you'd see that she is our own China Cat."

"Do you think so?" asked Mr. Mugg, hopefully.

"I'm sure of it!" declared his daughter. "Oh, if I only had a little soap and water."

"We can let you have some, lady," said the sergeant. "You may take the cat to the washroom and clean her."

This Miss Geraldine did. Under the stream of water, when some soap had been rubbed on the China Cat, a great change took place. Off came the grime of the smoke! Off came the spots of sticky molasses! Off came the soiled marks made by Jeff's dirty hands! The White Cat, not coming to life while Miss Geraldine had her, of course got no soap in her eyes, as would have happened if she had been real.

Soon all the black, the grime, and the dirty spots were washed away. Geraldine dried the China Cat on a towel the sergeant gave her, and then held the plaything up in front of her father.

"Now isn't that our Cat?" asked Miss Geraldine.

Mr. Mugg looked carefully over the tops of his glasses. He ran his hands through his hair and then through his whiskers, and then rubbed his hands together.

"Why—er—yes—er—my dear—that is our China Cat!" he said. "We'll take her right back to the store! Oh, I'm very glad to get her back. Thank you, very much," he said to the police sergeant.

"You are welcome," replied the officer. Then Geraldine and her father hurried back to the toy shop, carrying the China Cat.

As for the white pussy, you can imagine how glad and happy she was to be clean again. Nothing else mattered for the time, and she would have mewed out a song if she had been allowed to do so. But of course she could not.

"Put her in the window," said Mr. Mugg, when he and his daughter reached the toy shop. "That little girl who was going to buy her may see the Cat and come in for her."

So the China toy was again put in the show window of the shop, which had been cleaned and put to rights after the fire. In the same window was some doll's furniture, and on the bureau was a looking glass. The China Cat caught a glimpse of herself. She was as clean and white as a new snowball.

"Oh, how glad I am!" she said to herself.

She looked all around. There in the window with her were most of the toys she had known for a long time. They did not seem to have been burned or scorched by the fire. In fact, though some of his playthings were damaged, Mr. Mugg did not, of course, put any of these in his show window.

Near the China Cat was a Jumping Jack, a Jack in the Box, the Talking Doll, a Policeman and a Fireman—not the same Policeman and Fireman who had been in the basement, but some just like them. Throughout the store was a smell of smoke; but this could not be helped.

The China Cat would have liked very much to speak to some of the other toys, but she was not allowed to do so.

"But when night comes," she said to herself, "I shall have a chance. Then we can all talk about the fire. I wonder if any of my friends had such adventures as I had?"

But the China Cat did not get the chance she hoped for. That very afternoon, the same day that she had been put in the show window, a little girl and a lady came to a stop outside the toy shop, to look in through the glass.

"Oh, Aunt Clara! See!" cried the little girl. "There is the China Cat you were going to buy for me! Mr. Mugg thought she was smashed in the fire, but she wasn't and here she is. Oh, please take me in and get me the China Cat!"

"Very well, my dear," said Aunt Clara. "I promised you the toy and you may have her."

The China Cat heard what was said, and, looking out of the window, she saw the same nice little girl who had once held her in her hands.

"Oh, I hope nothing happens this time," whispered the Cat. "I should like to live with that nice little girl."

"We have come for the China Cat, Mr. Mugg," said Aunt Clara, as the toy man came forward to wait on his customers. "We called right after the fire, but everything was so upset we did not come in."

"Oh, wasn't that fire dreadful!" sighed Mr. Mugg, raising his hands. "I thought my whole place would burn! But the firemen carried out a lot of the toys, and though this white China Cat was stolen, I have her back. So you want her, do you, little girl?" he asked.

"Oh, I want her very much!" said Jennie Moore, and the China Cat was placed in her hands.

"Now for some new adventures," thought the toy, as she felt the nice little girl softly rubbing her white head.

CHAPTER IX

AN OLD FRIEND

Jennie Moore's aunt paid Mr. Mugg for the white China Cat, and the little girl carried the toy out of the store, not even waiting to have wrapping paper put around her.

"She is afraid the China Cat may be caught in another fire, or that something will happen," laughed the aunt, as she followed her niece.

"Oh, I hope there will never be another fire!" exclaimed Mr. Mugg, as he bowed his customers out of the door. "I can't imagine what started this one. But I am glad the China Cat is safe, though she did get very dirty."

"She is clean now," said Jennie, turning her China Cat over and over, and not finding a speck of dirt on her.

"What are you going to call your China Cat, Jennie?" asked Aunt Clara, when they had almost reached the home of the nice little girl.

"I will call her Snowball," was the answer. "She is white, just like a snowball."

"And from what Mr. Mugg said, I imagine she was as black as coal after the fire," laughed Aunt Clara. "Well, I am glad Snowball is clean and white now, and that you at last have her. Take good care of her and don't drop your cat, for I think she will break easily."

"I'll be careful," promised Jennie.

"Oh, how different this is from the time when that terrible black boy, Jeff, had me," thought the China Cat, as she was taken into Jennie's home. There the rooms were bright, cheerful and sunny, with soft carpets on the floor and beautiful ornaments all about.

"Now we'll have some fun, Snowball," said Jennie to the China Cat, as she set her toy down on a table, while she took off her hat and coat, for it was winter and the weather was cold, even though it did rain at times, instead of snow.

"You will not have to be afraid of a flood here, Snowball," went on Jennie, "for we are far from the river."

"Thank goodness for that," thought the China Cat, who heard all that was said, though she could not move when Jennie, or any one else, was looking at her.

Jennie played with the China Cat all the rest of that day. Once the nice little girl dressed the China Cat up in doll's clothes and pretended she was a doll.

"Though I cannot say I liked that," said the China Cat, telling her adventures afterward to her friend, the Talking Doll. "The clothes sort of tickled me. But Jennie was so kind and good I did not want to make a fuss."

When evening came Jennie put her China Cat away in a closet in her room, where there were many other toys. At first it was so dark that the China Cat could see nothing, but, after a while, she saw where some light came in through the keyhole, and then Snowball could look about her. The light that came through the hole was not daylight, for it was now night, and Jennie was going to bed. It was the light from a little lamp that burned all night just outside Jennie's room, and the China Cat was glad of that, for by the gleam she was able to see her way around the closet.

"Thank goodness now I can move and stretch myself a bit," said the China Cat, speaking out loud, in toy language. "I haven't had a chance to do as I pleased since just before the fire."

"What's that about a fire?" suddenly asked a voice just behind the China Cat. She looked around the shelf on which she sat but could see no one, though a Wooden Doll, with funny, staring eyes, was looking straight at her.

"Did you speak?" asked the China Cat of the Wooden Doll.

"No," was the answer. "Though I was just going to. I'm glad you have come here to live with us. You'll like it here. Jennie is such a nice little girl."

"We're all nice!" cried the same voice that had asked about the fire.

"Who is that?" asked the China Cat, for, as before, she saw no one.

"Oh, it's probably Jack," answered the Wooden Doll. "He's always playing jokes."

"Jack who?" asked the China Cat.

"Jack Box," answered the Wooden Doll. "He's one of those funny, pop-up Jacks in a Box, and he's always trying to fool some one. I suppose, because you are the newest toy to come here, that he is playing a trick on you."

"No trick, Wooden Doll! Just trying to be friendly and jolly—that's all!" went on the voice, with a laugh, and from a box near the China Cat sprang one of the queer Jacks that have such a sudden way of appearing.

"Oh! How you surprised me!" mewed the Cat.

"That's just my way! Can't help it! Have to jump when my spring uncoils!" said the Jack, with a broad grin on his face. "Let's have some fun!" he went on. "It's our chance to make believe come to life, now that Jennie has gone to bed. Sweet child. I like her, don't you?" he asked Snowball.

"Yes. But how you rattle on," said the China Cat. "You don't give one a chance to think."

"Yes, Jack is always like that," said the Wooden Doll.

"Well, let's have some fun," went on Jack. "What do you say to a game of tag?"

Leaning over, which he could readily do, as the coiled spring inside him was so easy to bend, Jack touched the China Cat. But Jack must have leaned too far, or too suddenly, for he brushed the Wooden Doll to one side.

"Oh, look out!" she cried. "You have knocked me off the shelf! Oh, there I go!" and the Wooden Doll fell straight down!

"Now you have done it!" mewed the China Cat.

"I hope her neck isn't broken," said a tiny Celluloid Doll. "Oh, what an accident!"

"I—I didn't mean to do it," said Jack sadly. "I'll go down and pick her up."

"Hush! Keep quiet, all of you!" suddenly mewed the China Cat. "Some one is coming!"

On the other side of the closet door, in the room where Jennie slept, the toys could hear the voice of the little girl calling:

"Aunt Clara! Aunt Clara! Come here! There's something in my toy closet. I heard a noise! Maybe that colored boy is trying to get Snowball, my China Cat."

The China Cat Gazed Out of the Window. The China Cat Gazed Out of the Window.

"Nonsense, Jennie. You imagined it, dear. Go to sleep now," replied her aunt, coming in from her room and turning up the light.

"No, I didn't imagine it," declared Jennie. "I heard a noise in my closet. Please look, Aunt Clara."

So Aunt Clara opened the door, and there she saw the Wooden Doll on the floor. The Doll had fallen on some felt slippers and so was not in the least hurt.

"There it is," said Jennie's aunt. "Your Wooden Doll fell off the shelf. You couldn't have put her far enough back."

"Oh!" murmured Jennie sleepily. "I'm glad she wasn't broken, and I'm glad my China Cat is all right."

Then Jennie went to sleep again, but she never knew, nor did her aunt, that Jack had knocked down the Wooden Doll.

"Behave yourself now, Jack," said the Celluloid Doll, when the toys were once more left alone. "If you play, let it be some easy game, like telling stories or riddles."

"All right," agreed Jack. "Suppose the China Cat tells us the story of the fire and the flood."

So the China Cat did, just as they are set down in this book. And after that the toys played guessing games, and told riddles until it was time for them to stop, as morning was at hand.

Jennie awakened early, and got her China Cat from the closet.

"You are one of my nicest toys," said the little girl. "To-day I am going to put you in the front window where you can see everything, and where the other children can see you."

So after breakfast the China Cat was set in the front window of the house, while Jennie sat near in a chair reading a book of fairy stories. After a while Jennie was called away to help her aunt, and the China Cat was left alone. For the first time that day she could look about as she pleased, moving her head and stretching her paws, as no one was in the room.

The China Cat gazed out of the window toward the house next door, and what was her great surprise to see in the front window there an old friend.

"Well, I do declare!" mewed the China Cat to herself. "How did he get here? Oh, if I could only speak to him! See, he is bowing to me! Oh, isn't this just wonderful!"

CHAPTER X

THE GLARING EYES

Snowball, the China Cat, was so excited that she felt she must really jump out of the window and go across the yard to her old friend, when Jennie, the little girl, came back into the room. Of course the China Cat had to be very still and quiet then.

"Oh, Joe has his Nodding Donkey in the window!" exclaimed Jennie. "That's a sign he wants me to come over and play with him. I'll go and ask Aunt Clara if I may go!"

Out of the room sped Jennie again, and the China Cat, who had heard what the little girl said, mewed to herself:

"At last I shall have a chance to see the Nodding Donkey again." For it was this old friend at whom the China Cat had looked through the window, watching him nod his head.

"Yes, Jennie. What is it?" asked Aunt Clara, as the little girl called to her.

"Please may I go over and see Joe?" begged Jennie. "He has set his Nodding Donkey in his front window, and that means he wants me to come over. He always does that when he wants me. I'll take my new China Cat over to see him."

"Very well, dear," agreed Aunt Clara, and a little later Jennie was crossing the yard, carrying Snowball under her arm. The China Cat was very glad that she was going to be taken to see the Nodding Donkey, with whom she used to live in Mr. Mugg's store.

"I'm glad you came over, Jennie," said Joe, as he opened the door for the little girl. "What have you?"

"My new China Cat, named Snowball. I brought her over so she could play with your Nodding Donkey."

"I guess maybe they know one another," said Joe. "They came from the same store, you know."

"Oh, so they did!" exclaimed Jennie.

"I have a toy wagon," said Joe. "I'll hitch my Nodding Donkey up to it, and we'll give your China Cat a ride."

"Oh, that will be fun!" cried Jennie. "Only don't upset her, for if she falls out she may break off her tail."

"I'll be careful," promised Joe, and then he and Jennie had a lot more fun with the Nodding Donkey and the China Cat. They were just thinking up another game to play when Joe cried:

"Here come Dorothy with her Sawdust Doll and Mirabell with her Lamb on Wheels."

"I should like to meet those toys," mewed the Cat to herself. And, a little later she did, as two other little girls came in to play with Joe. Then along came Dick, who was Dorothy's brother, and he brought his White Rocking Horse, though it was rather a large and heavy toy to carry. And Arnold, who was Mirabell's brother, brought along his Bold Tin Captain Soldier and his men.

Now began a very gladsome time for Snowball. She lived in a fine house, with a dear little girl for a mistress, and she had no more troubles.

Thus Winter passed and Spring came, with warm, sunny days when the children could play with their toys on the porches. One day Joe took his Nodding Donkey and went over to call on Jennie and her China Cat. But just as Joe was going up the porch steps he heard a hand organ down the street.

"Maybe there's a monkey with that hand organ!" said Joe to himself. So, without stopping to ring the bell, or letting Jennie know he had come to call, Joe set his Nodding Donkey down on the porch and ran out of the yard.

And now I must tell you what happened. The hand organ was quite a distance from Jennie's house, and it took Joe some little time to reach it. While he was gone, having, as I said, left his Nodding Donkey on Jennie's porch, along came sneaking Jeff, the colored boy.

Jeff's family had moved back into their basement tenement after the flood, and Jeff was the same dirty, careless colored boy as before. He, too, had heard the music of the hand organ down the street and he wanted to see if there was a monkey.

But as he was passing Jennie's house he looked toward the porch, and there he saw Joe's Nodding Donkey.

"Oh, golly!" whispered Jeff to himself, "dis yeah is mah chance! I kin git dat Donkey, suah!"

Sneaking along, Jeff softly opened the gate and went into Jennie's yard. On tiptoes he approached the porch where the Nodding Donkey was slowly shaking his head up and down.

"Dis yeah suah is a fine toy!" muttered Jeff. "It's a heap sight better dan de China Cat I got at de fire! I'll take dis Donkey!"

Jeff reached the porch and stretched out his black, dirty hands to take the Nodding Donkey. But, as he did so, the negro boy happened to look up at a side window, and there, on a table behind the glass, sat the China Cat!

The China Cat had big, staring eyes, and now because of the way the sun shone on them, they seemed to glare straight at Jeff. They even seemed to open wider, and move and blink, did those glaring eyes of the China Cat.

Jeff stood still and pulled back his hands that had been about to take the Nodding Donkey.

"Oh, golly!" he murmured. "Oh, dey's lookin' straight at me, dey is! Dat's de China Cat I tooked from de fire, an' she must have come to life! Oh, I dassn't take dat Donkey while she's glarin' at me wif dem big eyes! Oh, I's skeered, I is!"

With that Jeff turned and started on a run out of the yard. The Nodding Donkey, who had been very much afraid he was about to be stolen, was so thankful he did not know what to do. And the China Cat, who had feared that her friend was about to be taken from her, kept on staring as hard as she could.

Jeff ran faster. He gave one look back over his shoulder to see if any one might be chasing him, and he caught sight of the Cat's eyes again.

"Oh, golly!" cried Jeff.

At that moment his foot caught in a loose board of the walk, and down fell that bad boy Jeff with a bang, bruising knees and his nose and his chin.

"Ouch!" cried Jeff, as he got up and limped away.

"It serves him right," said the China Cat to herself, "for trying to take my friend, the Nodding Donkey."

"I guess you won't come back here in a hurry," said the Donkey to himself, as he saw Jeff going off down the street as fast as he could go. And the colored boy never did.

Joe came back, after having seen the hand organ and the monkey, and Joe carried his Nodding Donkey into Jennie's house. There the children played with their toys.

"How can I ever thank you?" said the Nodding Donkey to the China Cat. "With your big, glaring eyes you saved me from that colored boy."

"I am glad I did," mewed the Cat. "I didn't want you to be taken away from me. You are the best friend I have."

"I am glad you think so," brayed the Nodding Donkey. "I had another very good friend in the workshop of Santa Claus, at the North Pole, but I have not seen him for a long time."

"Who was that?" asked the China Cat.

"He was a Plush Bear," answered the Nodding Donkey. "A most wonderful Plush Bear! When he was wound up he moved his head and his paws and he growled as natural as anything."

"Oh, tell me about him!" mewed the China Cat. "Tell me about the Plush Bear."

The Nodding Donkey was just going to do this when Jennie and Joe came into the room and the toys had to remain quiet, not even talking.

But I happen to know the story of the Plush Bear, and it is to be the very next one I tell you of these Make Believe Stories.

Of course Snowball had many more good times while she lived with Jennie, which she did for many years. She often had fun with the Nodding Donkey and other toys.

One day Joe came over to Jennie's house, carrying his Nodding Donkey, a toy which was seldom out of his arms.

"Oh, Jennie!" cried Joe, "let's have a picnic in the woods for our toys. I'll take my Donkey, you can take your China Cat and I'll get Dorothy, Dick and the others to bring their toys."

"Oh, what fun to have a Toy Picnic!" exclaimed Jennie.

And the Nodding Donkey and the China Cat looked at one another most happily. They liked good times. The Toy Picnic was a great success, and how the boys and girls did laugh when the China Cat fell into the brook!

"But it doesn't hurt her," said Jennie, "and I was going to give her a bath, anyhow, 'cause I got some sticky candy on her tail."

The Cat, herself, was glad to be washed and clean, and here we must leave her, having fun as she is with the other toys.

THE END